TAR

A **BIRD PROBLEMS** STORY

M.A. **GOOSE**

TAR
Copyright © 2017, Bird Problems
All rights reserved

Bird Problems
www.birdproblems.ca

Book design by Kyle Flemmer

ISBN-13: 978-1979805285
ISBN-10: 1979805288

Bird Problems is a progressive metal quartet from Montréal consisting of Joseph Anidjar (guitar), Max Laramee (bass), Daniel Smilovitch (drums), and Michael Smilovitch (vocals).

M.A. Goose has close ties to the band, though he prefers to remain shrouded in mystery.

Check out "TAR" on Bandcamp, iTunes, Spotify, or Google Music, or purchase at **birdproblems.bandcamp.com/album/tar**

TAR
A **BIRD PROBLEMS** STORY

Preface	5
1. Invocation	7
2. Claw	10
3. Quarantine	16
4. Lush	22
5. Right of the Infected (ROTI)	32
6. da$$munny	41
7. Unlucky Me	44
8. Wasteland	56
Interlude	71
9. Succulent	77
10. Imbroglio	91
11. Ashes	96

Preface

Hello, and welcome to the inaugural Bird Problems novella. I just wanted to quickly clarify a few things before we begin. First, this isn't one of those stories that's meant to be read while you are listening to the album. You are welcome to do this, but I expect it would be overwhelming, detracting from the respective works. Each chapter in this volume corresponds to a song, and clarifies what is happening in the overarching story. The album's lyrics are not always so explicit, instead attempting to capture a certain feeling or event that is happening within a chapter. The lyrics and stories are therefore in dialogue, and you will find many references from one to the other throughout these works. I made the volume this way because I approach art as a puzzle. I adore analysis; picking apart a story, a line, thinking about why something is structured or phrased the way that it is. In writing *Tar* I tried to both abide by the puzzling nature of the literature I love, while deviating from it where possible in an attempt to make something vaguely novel.

Well, that's enough of that. Thank you for granting me a paragraph of explicit masturbatory pretension. I hope you enjoy reading and listening to *Tar*.

Stay classy,
M.A. Goose

1. Invocation

as told by Crisis, who struggles to forgive himself

I sing of method, and discerning eyes – how bad science drove some mad and turned others cruel. You can call me Crisis, unassuming leader of the scorned. I approach you modest, broken and estranged, descriptive at best. I could start by describing my surroundings, that's usually how these things go. I've had a good run, and I want you to know how it happened. There were others too, maybe they'll be here soon and you can meet them. Until then I can take on their voices, assume their perspectives in order to deliver a richer experience to you. Because this is all about you, really. We are in a hotel, it appears, or what is left of one. The entrance has crumbled and the windows are barred; I don't think there's any way in or out. I haven't tried very hard to leave, admittedly, I deserve to be here, and as I said, I've had a good run.

8 | TAR

I could tell you about the fractured and rotting mirror, and the pieces of it that lie scattered around me like reflective confetti after a piercing celebration. I could show you my veins, tinted black. I could show you what's under my skin, and you'd see how I am different from you. My wounds billow and smoke. My blood is heavy and black, like tar. My disease has filled me with sludge, and I feel heavy and warm and vile, and you made me feel like this, and we only have ourselves to blame, and there's nothing wrong with that, and there's nothing wrong with me, and there's everything wrong with me.

In a cave, curiosity wounds the proverbial cat.
Warm water, a man rallies my supporters. He is smarter than me, but less charismatic.
My home is a prison, it stinks of loss.
A man on a podium talks about good science and is assaulted.
Time slows, chaos hovers.
Hell unfolds, and people of warring opinions are indiscriminately punished.
I run away from a conflict and leave those who believed in me to suffer.

*I am happened upon and do bad things but feel
    incredible.*
*Someone is put on trial. I am the judge, the jury, and
    the accused.*
*Someone far better than me does everything I wanted
    to do, far better than I ever could.*

Pardon the obscurity, but I wouldn't want to ruin too much. Ruin is delicate, and just enough must be ruined in order to advance. They'll be here soon, I know it, and you'll meet them all. Thank you for being here. Bless you for coming along with me.

2. Claw

featuring Epsilon, an argumentative and the first infected

A drop of water slithered down the cave's right arm. Perhaps it was the cave's left arm. The friction made by waterdrop upon cavernside produced a sound too quiet for humans to hear. Deeper in the cave were other sounds; voices arguing, and the rhythmic cracks of shovels upon uneven ground. These sounds were audible to humans, and the voices belonged to Epsilon and Beefeater, neither going by their real names. The two men were joined by a third companion. She sat silently on a rock beside them, reading intently a work of nonfiction.

These voices floated through the cave in stale disagreement, and mingled with the sound of their shovels, rollicking off rockfaces and bouncing from cavern to cavern. Epsilon and Beefeater argued as they dug:

"The book obviously symbolizes knowledge," Beefeater began.

"I don't buy it," deflected Epsilon. "How can you take something like that for granted?"

"It's just an understood thing, books symbolize knowledge, just like caves symbolize the unknown, it's not such a stretch, it's intuitive," said Beefeater decisively, wrenching a shovelful of rock from the ground at his feet. Epsilon saw an argumentative opening.

"Aha," prefaced Epsilon, clearly communicating that Beefeater should prepare himself for the exploitation of an argumentative opening, "but intuition is entirely subjective by nature, so how can an author know the manner in which these hidden symbols of theirs will be extracted by these intuitive types of yours? Did they really choose to have their character drop everything and read that book at the height of the story's action, its *denouement*, not because that's what the character would actually do, but because, when extracted, the book symbolizes an important theme?"

"Well the two aren't mutually exclusive, the book can be both practical and symbolic."

"That's unfair, though. Okay, forget symbols, what if the story has inconsistencies, or shifts in tone, and it seems as if the book is saying two opposing things? How do I decide if its author is subversively portraying the theme of ambivalence or if they're just bad at storytelling?"

"Wait, which book are we talking about now? The book in the book? Who cares if it's ambivalent, we don't even get to read it."

Epsilon groaned, backtracking a little bit in his head while wrestling a particularly stubborn chunk of dirt from the ground with his shovel. He gathered his thoughts and continued.

"I'm obviously not talking about the book within the book, stop trying to undermine my points with asides."

"You're just digging yourself a hole here, buddy." Beefeater smiled beneath his soot-ridden bandana.

"Okay, I'm done with you. Get our friend over there to help us move this rock."

Beefeater (whose name, we recall, was not Beefeater) brought two fingers beneath his bandana into his mouth and exhaled precisely, emitting an unnecessarily loud whistling noise, considering the group's proximity to one another and their being in a cave. The sound caught the attention of their silent companion, who put down her book and muttered something in vague agreement as she wandered towards the futile debaters.

The trio moved the rock with relative ease, an

action both practical and symbolic. The movement of the rock was practical in that the rock had been offering integral support to the cave's structure, which let out an ominous groan as soon as the rock was moved. The movement of the rock was symbolic as well, although what exactly it symbolized was unclear. It may have represented an establishment of direction and agency, or the instability caused by shifting worldviews, or even the displacement of male privilege (the rock was fairly phallic). Epsilon and Beefeater, along with their silent companion, were more concerned with the practical results of their moving the rock, as a now unsupported stanchion of stone came smashing down upon them. Two out of the three recoiled, and Epsilon faced the brunt of the collapse, his lower body crushed, and his legs all but lost. He produced a horribly inhuman noise.

A dark gas began to fill the chamber, gently emitting from the hollowed-out space the integral rock once occupied. Thick and inky air crawled through the facemasks of the explorers, stinging their eyes and burning at their throats. They began to cough, and recoiled further. Epsilon lay supine, his arms outstretched above his head, everything below his waist a mangled mess of dark gas, shattered bone, and boiling blood. Beefeater and the silent companion gathered themselves, then grabbed Epsilon by either hand, wrenching him free with newfound strength - surely the result of the epinephrine violently pumping through their bodies. Epsilon's body was torn loose, leaving most of both legs behind beneath the stone. His wounds seemed to cough a thick black substance. The silent companion tore at her shirt and applied it around the remains of Epsilon's legs as a tourniquet, still making use of the impossible strength granted to her by her body's frantic epinephral secretions. The cloth emitted a steam as it came into contact with Epsilon's blood, which did not so much flow as crawl, oozing across the cloth and around his legs with no particular agenda. The steam became darker, and as the explorers were helping Epsilon up to lean on their shoulders, he cried out. Shriller than before, and more human.

"What happened to the tourniquet?" Beefeater shouted over the hiss of the smoke.

"It's burning," replied the silent companion.

"Why the *fuck* is the tourniquet burning?"

The tattered remains of the burned-through piece of shirt fell uselessly to the ground. Beefeater tried to reapply it but found his hands stung with acidity upon touching the dark blood. He pulled his hand back to reveal a fresh welt. The substance was everywhere, puddles sizzled on the ground, and the smoke in the passageway became thicker with each passing second.

"Go," mustered Epsilon, who was feeling particularly human. The others took no time to argue and left him, admonished.

They had tried, thought Beefeater, though intention was bullshit, he reasoned to himself. Epsilon definitely wasn't the best guy, he thought, but recoiled. Epsilon didn't deserve this any more than anyone else. Beefeater and the silent companion emerged from the cavern with steaming wounds and burns from Epsilon's tainted blood, the jet-black substance absorbing heat from the sun, which berated their eyes.

Both were treated at a nearby hospital, where many breathed the dark, unprecedented fumes that emitted from their wounds. Their condition spread rapidly before it was understood, airborne and highly contagious. The infected were deported, throngs at a time, after several violent incidents. Somewhat uncreatively, we called it Tar.

3. Quarantine

as thought by Basil, a controversial scientist vying to be the new face of a blossoming revolution

Dr. Basil Hollister was taking a shower. His refusal to simply take shower pills like everybody else was controversial. Some called him a purist. Others called him a skeptic. A handful called him a bourgeois piece of shit. Anyone who was foolish enough to defend shower pills to Basil's face, or to openly criticize his cleaning ritual was met with Dr. Hollister's three-pronged argument*, a pitchfork of justification.

---

* One: alone time with one's own mind. We require the intimate time provided by a traditional shower to be forced to be alone with our thoughts, even if only for a short time each day. This forced mind wandering and introspection allows us to stay in touch with ourselves, and avoid becoming completely lost in what we do. Where many saw a waste of time, Basil saw a necessary moment of separation from doing; a momentary pensiveness. Basil had also read that people used to come up with important ideas in the shower all the time, that's what convinced him to look for a contractor to get one installed in his parents' house.

Basil's outlook was of course inherently privileged. The Hollister family could afford enough water that Basil could use it to wash himself. He also had his own room, a luxury that most entire families could not afford. A sense of sheer luck crossed Basil's mind as droplets of water danced across his imperfect skin, dipping in and out of crevices leftover from picked-at pimples. He scrubbed his hair, which was dark and particularly unremarkable. "Bless you for inviting me to speak," he thought, and began running through his speech for the umpteenth time.

The young doctor continued his mental rehearsal as he stepped out of the shower and made his way back to his room. He lay on his bed, naked, and made note of the weight of his body upon the surface. His thoughts trailed

---

Two: acceptance of the physical self. Washing oneself is an intimate and crucial part of accepting the body and the self as a whole. Without a chance to strip away the fabric of our everyday lives we easily lose touch with what is underneath.

Three: the lack of longitudinal studies. Shower pills simply hadn't been around for long enough for anyone to know what the long-term effects were. Sure, there was nothing explicitly toxic in them, Basil conceded. That being said, just because the shower pills were virtually harmless in their contents didn't mean that they weren't having a massive impact on the way that people were developing. In Basil's professional opinion, taking away five meditative minutes per day from an entire society was bound to cause ripples in the mind, and affect the way people think across generations. Time would tell.

off, leaving the remainder of his speech to float and sputter away into some remote corner of his psyche. He looked over at a poster on the otherwise sparse wall before him. It was an old promotional poster for the Radical Altruists, from the early days of the Tar outbreak. "CRISIS IS CALLING" it said, printed in a blocky, black font upon a psychedelic post-apocalyptic backdrop ripe with rainbow-tinted explosions and gore.

They hadn't chosen the name Radical Altruists for themselves, the original name was more tasteful, but as with many things tasteful, it didn't stick.

Basil took pride in his being a fan of the RA before they had become cool again. The political group had been quite fashionable when Basil was a teenager; speaking to the disenfranchised and the bored, pairing politics with music and psychedelics. Terrified analysts had called it "the ultimate culmination of young people not giving a shit".

The RA had been led by Elliot Mackenzie during its heyday, a man who had his name legally changed to "Crisis" as a form of protest. An identity strike of sorts. Crisis was passionate, eccentric, and loud, hence he was able to quickly rally thousands of the disenfranchised to his side. This man was surely a narcissist, taking incredible pride in his appearance and actions. It was genuine, though.

He truly believed that he was the best man for the job and, though self-appointed, he wasn't far off. In truth, he was the fifth best man for the job. The top four were indisposed as a poet, an X-ray technician, a bus driver, and a petty thief, respectively.

To add to his eccentricity, Crisis was a tetrachromat: he had an extra cone in his eye compared to typical people and could allegedly see millions more colours than average. Under his rule, the Radical Altruists hosted massive, indulgent galas with lavish musical performances. Hosts circulated the events with tiny psychedelic hors d'oeuvres, containing just enough psilocybin to lightly tickle one's perception.

Basil watched it all happen, noted what Crisis was doing, how he methodically moved between crowds, greasing up each component, keeping his social engine slick and humming along, spewing fumes out in his path. But Basil didn't care. He knew all the tricks and fell for them all the same. He gave in to the mania. Crisis was worshipped as though he were a god. At least something good could come of this obsession. At least something could finally change for the better.

The RA's main agenda was the condemning and overturning of what they referred to as a "Passive War." The Tar virus was so poorly understood that the infected, along with anyone who came into contact with them, were indiscriminately moved to the dry outskirts of the quarantined city centers. These neglected areas were dramatically referred to as the "Wasteland."

The enduring issue was that nobody cared. Millions had seen the videos leaked by the RA of the Wasteland's horrifying conditions. They were disgusted and outraged, the people claimed, but life had gotten so much better since the deportations. There was more work and water to go around, wages were raised, rooms crammed with fifteens now housed more reasonable tens. Basil felt sick at how little of a shit everyone gave. He was a hypocrite, he thought, enjoying his bourgeois shower in his parents' house.

Rampant complacency towards this "Passive War" frustrated enough people for the Radical Altruists to gain a decent amount of traction and respect. The group, comprised mainly of scientists and skeptics at first, called into question the real functional danger of Tar. They believed that Tar did not inherently cause aggression. The RA disseminated explanations for violent outbursts by the infected, blaming discrimination and external hostilities. They harbored infected individuals in underground labs for research, published papers anonymously. The whole aesthetic of the movement had appealed greatly to Basil, who lived comfortably enough to openly question the deportations. He became obsessed with Crisis and the RA, attending rallies and meet-ups, and carefully studying their publications.

Crisis was unceremoniously placed under house arrest after spearheading a demonstration that went slightly too far, leaving a vacuum in the RA's leadership. The movement lost momentum for several years, and hadn't done much in almost a decade. Basil, still naked in his bed and staring at the ceiling, started to practice his speech again. The general assembly was to begin in three hours, and Basil would be giving his public address as a candidate to be the new leader. He looked back over at the old poster and shuddered. Basil, once again distracted from his speech, began to talk himself up. He would be everything that Crisis failed to be. He had the scientific background, the private research facilities, and his work was looking promising. He would show the world the truth about Tar, and be showered in adoration.

4. Lush

as told by Crisis, a resident prisoner in his own home

Now this is hardly fair.

"Any progress on the paperwork?" I want to ask, but this would make me seem invested in going to see the kid's speech, which I'm not. So I play it cool, sit down on the carpeted floor of the office, and say, "sup." All lower case with a period at the end. Not a question so much as a statement. It barely warrants a response and Cass is too proud to humor me with one. She looks down at me and I can feel her silently scoff. She must know that I am invested, clever as she is.

Cass (whose real name is Cassandra), is my personal security guard, handler, and illicit lover. Well, illicit fucker at least. Love hasn't been discussed, and I will assume it will not be for the sake of the coherence of our arrangement. Fucking Cass in the one blind spot unreached by the surveillance cameras across my house has become so routine that it's barely enjoyable anymore. At first it was great, finding one another in that calculated corner, creating an excuse to move the tasteless ceramic mass that bisected that tiny alcove of anonymity in order to create barely enough space for our bodies.

Of course, as subtle as we are disappearing off into our cramped, un-filmable alcove, anyone who took the time to even glance at my surveillance cameras knew exactly what was going on. Nobody really cared too much. Everybody knows I'm not dangerous, I was arrested to keep up appearances. Cass also commands so much respect around her department that nobody would dare call her out. Everyone just goes about their business, and as long as there isn't any physical video evidence of us fucking that could be leaked, everything is just fine. Relatively.

My day-to-day is miserably banal. Illicit alcove sessions included. We haven't had one today, since Cass is working on calling in favors for me, and I don't miss it at all. It's almost liberating not to have it, shakes things up a bit.

"You should be happy to be stuck inside during winter," they told me.

"But the sun is out, and look at all that not-quite-snow, not-quite-water out there," I reply.

"You mean slush?"

"I've always found that term to be derogatory."

Cass is busy working on getting me special permission to leave the house, on the grounds that it would only be to attend Basil's speech at the RA gathering. Lots of logistics – transportation, security and such – so she's holed up in my office while I wander about my hollow abode like an unsupervised toddler. I predict that watching Basil speak will likely trigger an ungodly internal emulsion of liberation and humiliation. If the authorities predict something similar, I gather it will make them more likely to allow me to go. Seems like an even enough trade: they'd love to see me humiliated a bit, and I need some fucking air.

I feel myself slipping. Home confinement has changed me. What an oxymoronic term. It stops being a home once you're not allowed to leave. Cage confinement, they should call it. I wander across the hall into my room and stumble over a mass of neglected clothing that Cass hasn't had time to pick up today. I kind of like the convenience of having all my clothes indexed upon the ground for a quick grab. It drives Cass insane. I crawl into my unmade bed and allow myself to recline as I drift back to a time of constant sensation and essence, and experience a vivid inner retelling of a stroll on a late winter's day:

As I step outside, my eyes are assaulted. I pull down my eyelids, like personalized drapes, but stalks of sunlight breach their surface. Instead of darkness I am treated with inferno, a private symphony of reds beneath my eyelids that no one else will ever know. I feel and I smile, glad that we cannot yet record and reproduce experience – the integrity of being would be lost.

I open my eyes and the light's barrage becomes more endurable. Each time the sun's rays strike me I become more resistant to them, like a man mercilessly beaten in reverse, standing up unscathed, and bidding his attacker a naïve farewell. I revel in my body's automatic adjustment to these conditions.

Empowered, I begin to examine the sun's surroundings. The moon has eagerly made its presence known today, its half complete frame sitting defiantly upon a backdrop of glowing sky. Unfazed by daylight, it mocks me as I continue to avert the sun's gaze.

I step out onto the street and hear a forgiving squelch as my boots sink slightly into the accumulated slush along the gutter. I take note of this, and with every step allow my body to resonate with the subtle movement the newfound resistance offers.

As I peel a foot up from the ground, I notice that I've

disrupted the patterns that passing vehicles have strewn across the muck throughout the day. Every step I take on this surface bears consequence. Every time I decide to move, I change the world, transform the universe.

I imagine the very first mechanical animal of the day, stumbling across the street this morning as it was piloted by an eager, average nobody. As it passed, it left a small, unique echo in the slush's impressionable surface. By this time of day, the echoes of so many perfunctory creatures, of countless separate lives, have been irreparably strewn together. They blend into cacophony – witness to the day's schizophrenic hum of exhaust fumes and private boxes. I no longer feel remorse for destroying these imprints. An equally overgrown pattern will be here tomorrow.

My inner ramblings of general disapproval keep me occupied until I've navigated myself across the road. My eyes have been fixated on the physical slush itself to the same degree that my mind has been fixated on what it says about the day's events. Once I notice this, I force my eyes back upwards like everyone else — looking straight and far ahead but expecting nothing. I get bored of this exercise pretty quickly and wonder how anyone could ever become so jaded as to have no desire to look around. I'm frantic, in sheer wonderment at everything that we've made, and everything that we haven't. A loud ringing noise pierces the air, curtly pounding at the gates of my fantasy. I wince and ignore it.

I notice a woman down the street walking briskly in my direction, her neck enveloped by a scarf of such intense colour that I can feel its undemanding warmth caress me from where I stand. Brilliant, it radiates comfort as it rests gently over her shoulders and slides slyly down into the dark folds of her winter jacket.

As she draws nearer, I notice that her eyes are fixed without remark on the bleached ground at my feet. I smile at her, becoming conscious of how my face looks as I wonder if she'll notice it. I curse the sun as I realize that I'm still squinting slightly, but it's of little consequence, my cursory attempt at human interaction goes unreciprocated, and the woman's eyes remain locked in place. The ringing comes again, the intrusive noise rudely resonating through the air before fading away. It startles me less this time.

I can only hope that I stirred a thought process in her, as she has done in me, but I'll never know if she even saw me. Then again, how many people have I passed who might have been thinking about me? Each word uttered, every jumbled interaction, any thought acknowledged or spurned could have been anything and everything else.

Every moment that we're conscious we make a choice, and every choice we make transforms who we are. As bitter winds assault me from the east, I struggle to find solace in my inability to experience all my potential lives. An infinite amount of these lives have passed me by. Is there beauty in limitation? Eye contact. It's as physical as it sounds, like a hug it can be comforting, or overwhelming, but it's always physical. The phone rings a third time.

I navigate myself to the corner of my room in which the phone is hidden away, tiptoeing carefully around the socks and shards of shattered flashback that lie scattered across the carpet. I pluck the phone from its perch and lightly toss it from my right hand to my left, catching it by the nostalgic chord.

There is a certain dead quality to the voice. "Please check in," it tells me in a raw and uneasy tone. The receiver sways lazily in front of my bowed head, the coiling cord clutched between my thumb and middle finger. "Please check in," the voice repeats, becoming agitated. The voice's blunt request is perfectly audible from the receiver's limp position, distant as it may be from my ear. I know better than to disregard the dour, disembodied demand any further.

"Ahem," I muster before attempting to construct

words, "restless hedonist, checking in." The phrase comes out a sputter, exercising the extent of my ability to fight back. Yesterday I said, "over-analyst," the day before, "cynical bastard." I have very little wiggle room when it comes to my correspondence with the authorities, but there seems to be a decent amount of leeway with respect to the manner in which I check in. All they really need is to hear my voice. "Your tongue feels uncomfortable in your mouth," I quickly tell the phone, consciously refusing to think of my tongue's comfort level.

"Fuck you," it replies, hanging up. I amuse myself, which is more important in my sort of situation than you might think.

All inconsequential dissent aside, my daily interaction with the voice leaves me drained. There is no subtlety to it, and it does nothing but remind me of my plight – a realization that starts in my mind and works its way down, through my chest, to the core of my gut. I know it's coming, and though I try to chase the reality of my situation from my head, my subconscious ensnares it and hides it somewhere inside of me. I begin to feel sick, undoubtedly a psychosomatic experience. Still, it impresses me how my fleeting fears and discomforts can make my body turn against itself. I can feel my heart beating in my stomach, disgusted by my predicament, shouting at me to fight. I love that we are hardwired for fear and recede into ourselves. Cowardice is a defense mechanism, though rarely treated as such.

"You should really try to humor them a bit more," Cass shouts from the office across the hall. "Maybe they'll let you out of here on good behavior"

"I love it here, why would I ever want to leave?" I reply, my voice shaking. Not impressive. Barely a facade. I used to be good at this sort of thing. Now my attempts at seeming 'comfortable' are about as convincing as two children stacked beneath a trench coat attempting to purchase pornography. Cass will have none of it and will certainly not be selling me any pornography, figurative or otherwise.

I grab onto one of the many rusted metal pipes running up across the wall next to the phone. Heat exchange occurs as the colder metal contacts my skin, both individual substances trying to split things evenly. My hand feels cold, as I imagine the metal would feel warm, if it were capable of such a thing. I continue to think about the exchange I've made with the pipe as I let it anchor me, and proceed to slide my body down until I'm sitting on the ground, in the corner, looking around myself.

The room is comically spacious, though the echoes of

old, fuller furnishings cannot be hidden. Tasteful imprints riddle the ground where leather couches once reclined, and the vague markings of bygone structures can be found in all corners of the room. It was all stale, eroded, doing me a disservice. Any subjectivity eludes me at this point, so the chances of my tastes matching up with those of designers and consumers seem thin, and there is rarely a furniture piece I feel has the integrity necessary to be placed in my cage. Because that's the only dignity I have left, right? Emptiness.

5. Right of the Infected (ROTI)

in which Basil presents his research on national television and makes a groundbreaking confession

I should get out more, it feels good.

I joke, of course. House arrest. I haven't the choice.

The DJ is playing something minimal, and dark.

The kid looks good up there, a bit nervous but that's to be expected. The music stops mid-song and Basil begins:

"Bless you for inviting me to speak…"

I'm sure his work is ground-breaking. Truly. I believe it.

I reach for an appetizer. Cass slaps my hand away. Playfully, but stern. She could fuck me up. I shoot her a knowing glance.

I'm not allowed any of the hors d'oeuvres here, it's in the terms of my house arrest, even though the "light recreational use" of psychedelics has been legal here for decades. These ones aren't as strong as we used to make them anyways, I bet. I'm sure they wouldn't even do anything to me.

There are lots of rules, always lots of rules for me to be allowed anywhere, the paperwork, dear lord, the paperwork it must have taken to get me here. I guess refraining from "lightly tickling my perception" is the least I can do to show my appreciation.

Everyone seems to be enjoying themselves, the crowd that is. He has fans, this Basil kid. Doing well for himself. Not like me though. He thinks too much.

Solid turnout, I've got to admit. I'm not sure I've ever seen the old HQ auditorium this packed.

"A bit excessive, no?" I ask Cass, gesturing by craning my neck on an angle towards my hands cuffed behind my back.

"Shut up and listen," she replies. Very stern, this one. I shoot her another knowing glance, but her eyes widen and saccade over to a nearby camera to inform me of its presence.

Right, this is all being televised. Historic event and all. Good fun, I guess. I should keep the knowing glances to a minimum if it's all to be on record though. She makes a fair point with her eyes, this one. I shut up and listen for a bit.

Basil continues:

"The human body is a delicate thing. We maintain a very specific internal temperature, hence the thermometer as an indicator of sickness. Tar is a condition that affects the human body in an unprecedented way. We responded with fear, treated it like a disease, sent our fellow humans away, and blocked off all communication. While I disagree with this reaction, I understand the place it came from. Change is scary, difference is scary. I think that Tar has so much to tell us about ourselves. We need to study it, understand how such a small amount can be so contagious. How it allows the body to withstand internal temperatures previously thought to be impossible. This is an incredible opportunity for science and medicine that has been stripped away by fear.

"The days of pleading are over. The days of rallying to bring the infected home on the basis of their humanity are over. Nobody listened. Nobody cared. So I went out to demonstrate, scientifically, my hypothesis – that this "disease" does not make people violent. It does not affect the brain. All of the bloodshed, red and black alike, was our own doing.

"The findings of our research, privately funded of course, have been robust, in that they are virtually nonexistent. We have been able to experiment on multiple individuals infected with the Tar virus, and have found absolutely no reason to suspect that the condition anything other than aesthetic. That is to say, while the virus certainly affects the appearance and viscosity of the blood, causing it to become darker and take on certain unprecedented properties – considerable heat and the production of a gas – the virus does not affect temperament. There is nothing biological about this sickness that is making people aggressive. This has been the resounding evidence found in all animal and human trials.

"You may then ask, why do we see so many reports of the horrible things that the infected do? Why did we see so many cases of infected fighting amongst themselves and with others outside of the city's Quarantine zone? I'm sure you've all seen the videos, horrific as they are…"

Nods and murmurs of assent.

"The infected, as they've been called, are a product of their mistreatment. We acted out of desperation without knowing what we were dealing with, putting people in situations where they needed to fight for their lives. I'm sure that any one of us here would act just as hostile and vicious if you were left out there to rot. It's human nature to adapt, and when treated like beasts, we act like beasts."

Basil pauses for a moment and his eyes wander around with less coherence than he'd probably like for slightly longer than is acceptable. He manages to wrest back control of his ocular muscles before anyone besides me notices.

"The kid's had a few too many appetizers," I whisper to Cass, who ignores me.

Dr. Hollister continues:

"The benign nature of Tar is hardly surprising for many of us. The founders of the RA have suspected from the beginning that this Passive War against Tar has been an excuse to trim the fat off our population. A way to deviate our attention from the actual problems our society has been facing. And now, before we can work to deal with our overpopulation, the strain on our resources and space, we must right the wrongs we have committed, and reintroduce the "infected" back into our society.

"This will be a challenge, I know, and I do not deny that many of those living in the Wasteland are extremely hostile. This is our own fault. I will spearhead a pilot program – the first of hopefully many recovery missions into the Wasteland. I will show the authorities that these people can be redeemed, rehabilitated, and reintroduced into our society. They may bleed black, but they still bleed. We all bleed. And it's high time we work at mending the wounds we've inflicted on these people, and spreading the truth about Tar. Thank you."

Uproar. Absolute mayhem. They love him.

Some sort of moderator takes to the podium and shakes Basil's hand. I imagine it is clammy.

"We will now open the floor to any questions," the moderator announces.

Wild animals, all of them. Reporters clambering over one another with inquiries. The mayhem is somewhat understandable; there are many questions to be asked about the kid's speech. Still, I'm sure there's a more coherent system that could be used. Perhaps they could line up. I guess it would be undemocratic to prevent people from fighting for a spot, though. They'll probably want to interview me after this too. My first public appearance in ages. I'll deal with it later.

There are several things that I'm wondering myself. Where's the kid finding these human subjects? It was virtually impossible to find any infected to study when I was in charge. The zero-tolerance policy used to be strict, and it has only gotten more stringent since. Anyone anywhere near an incident is promptly quarantined and deported. If someone who has been hiding the virus gets so much as a bad papercut in the same room as you, and you breathed that air, you'd be considered infected. That's all it takes, and you're air-dropped into the Wasteland.

It could be kind of fun, to be honest, fighting to survive out there. Might beat sitting at home every day under fucking house arrest. I have no idea what I'd do without Cass. Maybe I'd be fine, but the knowing glances are nice.

The first question is asked by a nervous bug-eyed hipster:

"You say that you've done extensive tests on the infected. We all know how tightly regulated infected experiments are. Q...questionable legality aside, do you ever worry about contracting Tar yourself? How often do you work with these sick people?"

Basil puts on a smile:

"You know," he begins, his voice echoing warmly through the auditorium, "almost every one of my advisors, lawyers, and investors would tell me to decline to answer that question. No good can come of it, they'd say. I can't tell you how many arguments I've had about this. About whether or not you deserve to know the details of what we've been doing. But you know what? If we keep you in the dark, then we're no better than the authorities that have been lying to us about this disease for all these years."

Right of the Infected (ROTI) | 39

The kid is sweating now, but still wearing his smile. He's got balls, I'll give him that.

"Monster-loving sap!" someone shouts, and the cameras swivel towards the source of the sound. The heckler is swiftly escorted out. That was really the best they could come up with? Sap? Seems like a waste. I look around and take note of a handful of people in particularly sober attire drizzled about the auditorium floor. I know undercover protestors when I see them. This isn't my first rodeo. Fuck I want an appetizer. I wonder if they still serve the ones with little bits of caramel in them.

"In order to publicly demonstrate to you all, right here tonight, that Tar is virtually harmless, I have performed a type of experiment on myself. In a controlled environment, I aspirated the fumes from a small cut in an infected research participant's arm." A rumble swells through the crowd. A splintering crash. "This was months ago," Basil continues, his voice growing louder and more uneasy as it competes with the noise of the crowd. "The disease has had time to incubate and I am completely temperamentally unaffected, having completed extensive tests." Basil is shouting at this point. A glimmer of light catches my eye, in the top rightmost corner of my field of vision. My eyes saccade to investigate and quickly lock onto the source of the sheen: a fractured bottle careening through the air towards the podium. It floats for a moment, beautifully hollow, jaggedly jade, and spinning as if in slow motion. Nobody else seems to notice.

6. da$$munny

in which a bottle of European cola floats through the air in slow motion

The moment stretches on. The distinctive green sheen of the floating bottle reveals it to be of the brand *da$$munny*, a European cola company which features aggressively self-aware marketing. They have acknowledged openly that they seek money, rather than world peace or the other shit that their competitors claim to stand for. And people go for it, their marketing works. I guess, admitting that you're scum is often more respectable than pretending you aren't. Deservedly so.

The company's CEO used to be one Jeremy Stone. He had started out as an artist and spearheaded *da$$munny Industries* as a sort of joke, one that swiftly got out of hand. Ironically, he was quite the philanthropist outside of his professional life. Unmarried due to ideology, he adopted a son, a legacy, and the duo graced the covers of many a tabloid.

Eventually, feature articles began to question the origin of Stone's son, rumors accusing the child of being infected, of Stone harboring him for a family that had long since been sent away. It certainly fit his alleged MO of being a decent human being. Rumors culminated in investigations, and without much warning, Stone and his son were sent away to the Wasteland.

da$$munny Industries was taken over by someone upon whom the irony of the whole operation was lost, but the profits were not, and *da$$munny* cola continues to pervade the modern world. I think about this all in an instant, quickly accessing the information, and then store it back away, focusing again on the floating bottle.

A splintering crash. Contact between glass and podium. Basil puts his arms up in defense, making an X in front of his face. The volume of the crowd's collective mumbling reaches a critical mass, then falls silent – dead silent – as everyone seems to realize in unison what I realized the second I saw that green glimmer out of the corner of my eye. Heads crane towards the speaker as he slowly lowers his arms. They appear unscathed.

The silence is gently shattered as the microphone begins to pick up a hiss, slowly increasing in volume. The source, a small abrasion above Basil's right eye begins to sputter and steam. A siren blares, doors slam shut. I catch myself smiling among the pandemonium.

7. Unlucky Me

as experienced by Basil, whose actions have condemned an entire auditorium to be deported

Basil Hollister felt empty. Was he in shock? If he was, shock felt nothing like it looked. The auditorium had fallen into complete disarray. Whomever it was who had thrown the bottle, everyone would pay for it. Some dealt with their fear internally, wrapping themselves up in little balls along the fringes of the auditorium floor. Others lashed out, outfitting their fear into rage, picking fights.

A struggle at the DJ booth was followed by the blaring of an easygoing, beach-like summer remix of a popular song. The dyssynchronous soundtrack billowed across the maddened auditorium. Were everyone in the room not doomed to be deported into uncertainty, the scene would have been quite comedic.

Basil noticed Crisis, who, conveniently already

handcuffed, was attempting to throw a gas-masked guard off of a burly female security guard, who was being handcuffed as well. He watched his idol topple over, contorted.

"Calm down!" the woman shouted. At the other guard? To anyone in particular? What a strange notion, that one should shout at someone to be calm. This crowd was the definition of implacable. Implacability incarnate.

A burly man in a red T-shirt, presumably in attendance to protest Basil's research, charged towards the podium, arms outstretched, pushing off of the bodies between Basil and himself while gaining momentum. Moving seemed an obscure concept to Basil, who was slowly working through the events of the previous minute. He had gotten stuck repeating "selfish, selfish, selfish" to himself in his head, which he soon decided was an inopportune use of his fleeting time. The burly redshirt had reached the podium when a meagre hipster with round glasses and a rattail rose to Dr. Hollister's defense, calling red T-shirt a fascist and raising lanky long-sleeved arms into an en-garde position.

The delicate and predictable notes of the summer remix, few and far between.

Basil stared through the one-sided scuffle meters before him. Was this really his fault? Should this have been expected? That he'd be attacked? Someone else might be at fault. The security, the assailant themselves, surely. You can't live your life in constant fear of someone throwing a cracked bottle at your face during a scientific revelation, can you? That's no way to live. But he had poisoned all these people. Intentions aside, he was the only reason that hundreds would now be locked up and shipped off, himself included. No, not poisoned, though, that was the point. Was nobody listening? They were all fine. The virus wasn't real, this was *bullshit*.

Crisis hummed along to the pop remix, several meters away from Basil, in the thick of it, cheek pressed against the polished auditorium floor, a guard's decisively gloved hand pressed down upon the opposite side of his head. Crisis wasn't particularly fond of the tune, but everyone else's almost militant distaste for it amused him more than the song turned him off, leading to an overall net gain of pleasure. He therefore never minded when it came on, and would smile to himself as others groaned.

The small scuffle before Basil had ended with the greasy hipster lying in a mangled heap at red T-shirt's feet. The victor now set his sights back to Dr. Hollister, who had not moved since being struck by that bottle, the small slash across his cheek still steaming and coughing up small clumps of obsidian gore.

Basil caught himself thinking about his parents as the fuming redshirt collided with his midsection, knocking the wind out of him and sending him over backwards, behind the podium. The burly man's eyes were bloodshot, their sanguine tinge growing darker as he breathed in the dark emanations from Basil's lacerated cheek, the red of his shirt growing brighter by comparison. The brute raised both arms above his head – one in a clenched fist, the other wrapped tightly around it.

Basil searched for that survival instinct inside him that was supposed to yell at him to move, to flinch, to roll out of the way of the violent downswing towards his face, but he found nothing. There was no desire for motion. He had too much to work through still, and his thought process had slowed to a melancholic slog. The bright red protester's downswing was inches from the doctor's delicate bespectacled face when it was interrupted by several of Basil's supporters rushing to his aid. The redshirt's blackening eyes widened in fury as he was wrested off Dr. Hollister and thrown backwards, falling awkwardly off the stage.

The young doctor was helped to his feet, and gazed out at the madness before him.

Protesters and supporters fought with words and utensils, everyone afraid, policemen in gas masks struggling through the crowd, batons dancing across backs and maws. A wave of groans and knocked-wind, a clear shift in power.

As a child, Basil had always been taught that he could do anything he wanted. The endless opportunity had weighed upon him more than any enraged protestor ever could have. What do you do when you're told you can do anything? How can you possibly choose? The phenomenon was known as analysis paralysis, Basil remembered reading about it during his undergraduate degree. It's a simple enough idea – when presented with too many options we can be rendered immobile, paralyzed. Too many options actually impedes our ability to make a decision. We get overwhelmed because we're not used to it, not programmed for it.

Was he seriously blaming his parents for this right now? The nerve. Basil chastised himself internally. It wasn't his fault he had been born into privilege, but it had filled his head up with these ideas that he could change the world. And if he hadn't tried... if he hadn't been so selfish... this crowd of people could go home to their families, live their lives. Was it selfish to want to lead? Someone has to do it. He wanted to help these people, right? Did his intentions bear any weight?

Surveying the scene before him, Basil couldn't help but wonder. Where would all these people be right now if he had gone to trade school, worked with his hands? Was his need to be the best, the smartest, the most important, was this really worth what had happened here tonight? One protester was clawing at a cop's gas mask, several others joined in. Nobody was thinking. Handfuls of folks remained at the fringes, rocking back and forth in fetal fright.

Tragically, one of the journalists was struck with an instance of profound inspiration: a song, fully formed. It was orchestral, lyricless, and it was all there, bursting suddenly into the journalist's mind in a single, inopportune moment. The journalist was too busy scampering away from dueling supporters, protesters, and police to hum the tune into his phone as he typically did in these rare but powerful instances of inspiration. As quickly as it appeared, the melody was gone.

The conflict persisted until a gas mask was successfully wrestled off a cop and he was promptly tackled and subdued by three of his coworkers. He would be sent away too. Noting the fallibility of the gas masks, more of the doomed and crazed attendees descended upon the police, forcing them to fall back out of the room, barring the door behind them.

A new gas, much thicker than the allegedly harmless dark fumes that sputtered from Basil's cheek, emanated into the room from under the barred door. Struggles became lazy, encumbered. Basil watched from the podium as supporters, protesters, journalists, caterers, cops, and security lost control of their facilities, crumbling to the ground. Warring philosophies turn irrelevant in mangled heaps across the floor.

Basil awoke as if dreaming, seated and held back by a harness – the sort that you pull down from above on roller coasters to lock yourself in. Facing him, a meter away perhaps, was an unconscious teenager in waiters' regalia, whom Basil recognized as having offered him an appetizer at the RA event. The guilt came rushing back like a physical blow, and Basil's stomach lurched. This kid had his whole life ahead of him. A second lurch – regret? No, this was different, purely physical. They were airborne, Basil decided. The doctor closed his eyes and picked up on the subtle hum of military-grade helicopter rotors.

A groggy survey of his surroundings revealed seats similar to his own stretching down a fluorescent hall, all of them full, some with familiar faces, many bloodied, some clearly infected, others seemingly unaffected. Basil estimated around half of the passengers were conscious, a few others seemed to be somewhere between consciousness and sleep. Crisis was seated in the row opposite to Basil, about seven seats to the left, only visible to Basil if one of them leaned forwards, which Crisis was now, hunched over, forearms on knees and eyes locked upon the aluminum flooring.

It was eerily silent, considering all of the preceding rage. The tranquility could have been due to a number of reasons. Basil had three theories.[*]

"We won, you know. I finished what you started," Basil said, looking across to Crisis. An incredulous grin. Crisis faced the aluminum flooring.

"Excuse me?"

---

[*] One: side effects from the knockout gas. The government guards had presumably used one of their undisclosed™ synthetic opioid gases on the crowd, which laid a sort of afterglow of placidity upon its victims.

Two: they had given up. There was nothing to be done at this point, Basil couldn't see any sort of authority figures. The presumable cockpit was blocked off by an industrial limousine-like divider. There was no handle or anything on their side. The tranquility could have been simple apathy.

Three: there was still the potential for conflict, but half of the passengers were unconscious. You can't have conflict without antagonists. It takes two to tango, and such.

"We won. My speech. Everyone saw it, there's no way they cut the feed in time."

"I'm sorry, so how did we win? Because last time I checked we were fucked."

"Now everyone knows the truth. About Tar. They won't stand for it." Basil said stubbornly.

Hearty laughter from Crisis.

"You're adorable." The ex-leader spoke. "You think you can just *change people's minds??* About something they *believe??* Nobody's going to admit they're wrong. Nobody's going to sacrifice all the free space they have now. Why would they? You changed *nothing*. All you've done is condemn a few dozen of your supporters and a catering crew to die."

"Hey, we were there to protest your bullshit!" shouted someone in a torn maroon shirt.

"I'm freelance," said someone in a jacket, quietly, to themselves.

"People will listen to *reason*," Basil muttered.

"They won't! People aren't reasonable. The furthest thing from it. And you can't blame them. You can't know what's true anymore. Here's an idea, let's talk about something relevant. The so-called Wasteland we're presumably being shipped off to *right now*. What have you heard about it?"

"We're fucking dead!" shouted one of the protestors. Crisis smiled.

"Now, now. Let the esteemed Dr. Hollister speak."

"It's tough..." Basil began, "because, well, I read a few interviews with people who made it back, right? And they said it was fine actually, it was a bit rougher than they were used to but really no rougher than a bad part of town, right? There's plenty of food that people left behind and everything, and if you're not worried about catching Tar...."

"Those interviews were fake! Plants! Inside guys! Everyone knows that," another protester shouted. Some others nodded in assent. "They fucking eat people out there, man. The Vultures, they call them. Just waiting around, sick and hungry and just waiting for a new batch of sorry fucks like us to get sent off to them. There are tons of reports of that too, the ones that survive that is, but they just get covered up. You wouldn't know with all your government money and your fucking *showers*." The man attempted to spit at Basil, but found his mouth unexpectedly dry and only managed to spittle a bit down his chin, which he then struggled to wipe off, having to contort his arm around the rigid harness over his shoulders.

"I heard the air is poison out there. Everything's dried

up," said someone from a corner. Crisis seemed satisfied with the interaction.

"Hmmm, seems like the jury's out on this one, Basil," he jeered. "You see, they seem pretty sure about their side of it all... and you... well you didn't sound too convincing. So who are you gonna believe?"

"I'd never believe something one-hundred percent, that's part of being a scientist," replied Basil. The doctor had to stretch his neck to keep Crisis in view.

"Then you can't hope to ever convince anyone of anything," Crisis replied, receding back into his harness, "because they don't think like you, and you can't make them think like you. Treating people like they're reasonable is a great way to get *fuck-all* done." Crisis sighed and reclined, moving completely out of Basil's field of view. He looked down to his right and winked at Cass, who was just coming to. She responded with a groggy glare signifying utter disgust. A hiss, and the harnesses came up. For a beat, some stretched, some started to speak, some stood up.

The titanium flooring fell out from beneath them, opening up down the middle. Crisis clutched at a receding harness, now inaccessible behind a panel, and fell through the floor of the air carrier, now two flaccid sheets swinging off to either side, and into the gaping maw of empty space;

ten, twenty feet maybe. They hit the ground with a series of sickening cracks in asymmetric intervals, like popcorn just before it starts to burn.

8. Wasteland

as told by Crisis, who abandons his followers and watches from afar

This space feels artificial. The air is thick, whoever said that had a point. Some bodies broke my fall, I think. What an awful noise. Less soft than you'd imagine, bodies, and you wouldn't imagine them to be very soft at all, would you? I clamber out from on top of the mound of moaning torsos.

Someone behind me shrieks. I don't know him, probably RA. They're softer than they used to be.

I turn around and notice the shrieking man is staring directly at a lion's chest – flowing mane around its head, a goat's besides, with a snake coming up around the concrete rear. *The Chimera*. It was an inspiring piece of sculpture work, not quite the same caliber as the classical works, but then again, what is? Eyes adjusting to the dark. The top half of the lion's sculpted skull seems to have melted away.

"Sulfuric acid," Basil says, just next to me it would seem. "From rain." The kid sighs. I feel a tinge of ambivalence.

All around me the fallen passengers are tending to legs and arms. Fractures, breaks maybe. I feel a bit energized. The moans of my followers elicit some guilt regarding my own well-being, I admit to myself.

We're outside, though! Kind of. I think there's a breeze. Dusty. I shiver, but don't mind. Maybe.

Another large sculpture features cherubs clambering on a sort of vague chunk of granite. The remains of their lips are pursed in a way that implies they were engineered at one point to spit out water. The birdpool-esque receptacle at their infantile feet confirms my suspicions.

Additional works of sculpture seem to stretch off across the courtyard in all directions, or at least as far as I can see unassisted at night in an unlit space, which is not very far at all. The ones I can see are entirely variant in terms of style. Some modern, postmodern, minimalist, right beside classical reconstructions that gleam with ancient similitude.

A large metal dome, shaped like a half-moon and horrifically rusted, stands defiantly beside what seems to be a small area devoted to sculptures inspired by the temple of Aphaea. It features nude soldiers bearing marble spears and shields, poised for battle.

One piece includes an imp-like figure with the top half of its skull missing, hollowed out. It's holding a book in one hand and a cup in the other. The goblet is held up and tilted backwards as if being poured from above into the creature's hollow skull.

I look closely at the stone book in the sculpture's hand. The parts which haven't dissolved look like mathematical formulas.

"Cute," says Basil, who seems to be following me around. "It's a formula for 'geluk'. That's Dutch for happiness."

"Or luck," I reply. And, I must admit to myself, I feel a bit of both happiness and luck, being outdoors and unscathed. I am relatively immune to the unappreciative moans surrounding.

"Where are we?" Cass now asks. She's limping over to us.

"Sculpture garden."

"No shit."

"Shhh!" Basil cuts in. "Look."

Lights, off in the distance. Flashlight, it looks like. The beams cut through the night and ricochet off various eroded statuettes. Faint voices too, complaining. It sounds like one of them says "deathtrap."

"Hey!" Basil attempts to shout and whisper at the

same time. He motions over to the rest of the group, most still moaning and tending to limbs. Some are wandering around and admiring the art. "Get down!" Another whisper-shout. It doesn't quite seem to rally anyone, until they notice the lights and hear the faint voices in the distance for themselves and decide that their maybe fractured ankle isn't worth dying over and they clamber over towards us, wincing.

"Follow me," says Cass, making her way back past *The Chimera* and towards the metal dome. Offering us refuge from the approaching strangers is the most practical thing this tastelessly grandiose piece has ever achieved, I almost say aloud. We huddle in the hollow artwork, about half of us fitting inside and the rest going around behind.

"Fuck" someone says, in a half-whisper. I look down.

"Fuck!" someone else says, slightly louder, in less of a whisper.

"Shhh!" Basil insists. I've always found shushing to be hypocritical. Someone vomits as quietly as one can vomit. Everyone starts making a bit too much noise in the ensuing discomfort. Someone else vomits. Corpses. Three or four litter the ground of our impeccable hiding spot.

Our eyes are assaulted by flashlight. I can't tell how

many people there are behind the beam, no more than five I think.

"Freshly fallen?" the one holding the flashlight speaks, his voice hoarse. He whistles ironically as though to say "I'm impressed," but the note falls flat after a second and the man erupts into a fit of coughing directed into the crook of his elbow. The figure waves a medium-sized blade in front of his flashlight so we can see it, but begins to cough again and pulls his arm back so as to cover his mouth.

"You've got some shitty luck, getting dropped off in the middle of Inn Between," the figure continues. "We're desperate as shit coming out here. These junkies can barely handle it." He motions back to the group behind him, they breathe deeply and mumble with what seems to be mildly intoxicated excitement.

The primary figure continues. "Now we've got a set of principles, for the most part. We don't want to trouble you. We're just here for those bodies in the dome. Now if you try to take them from us, then we'll have a problem." I can't make out any distinguishing features, past the light. Light's unfair like that, since they can see us all clearly, shielding our eyes, huddled together against the back of the rusted metal half-sphere.

"Take them," Basil manages to sputter. He does not

sound in charge, but at least he got it out. I think I could have spoken better. The man with the flashlight remains immobile, but nods and those behind him rush around and into the dome. I catch a quick glimpse of one's face, in the light, only really processing it after the fact, the image engraved into my retina. A teenage-looking girl, in a hoodie, lips stained black, with dark strands running down her chin. Mangled teeth jut from her gritted maw. The girl's hoodie has small burn-holes throughout, still steaming.

"Now don't be greedy. One apiece," the man with the flashlight announces, evidently the leader.

"Don't be greedy, one apiece," his followers echo back. Silence for a beat. People are shaking. I'm shaking. It's from the cold, I think, not fear. I'd like to think I'm desensitized to this sort of shit. Eyes are trained upon the ringleader's blade, which he holds in front of his flashlight, keeping us at bay.

"Are you...?" Basil tries to ask through his shakes.

"Vultures," the man confirms. "Not a name we chose... the original was far more tasteful, but you know, the tasteful ones never stick. We're not trying to hurt anyone. As the name suggests, we'd much rather pick at the scraps. The old way of thinking will bring you nothing but misery out here. Really rotten luck on your part, I've gotta say. If you knew the stories about this place…"

The Vulture leader tries to whistle again and gets about halfway this time before the tone's choked off by a deep hacking. He spits out a chunk of what looks like soot. It smokes pathetically upon the parched ground.

"Only three!" the hoodied girl shouts.

"Only three!" the others echo.

"Now, that's a real shame," the head Vulture speaks, calmly. "We're gonna need two more. Who's in charge here? We don't like doing this, but everyone's gotta eat. And you look like you've got plenty to spare."

Basil can't stop staring at the knife.

"Sorry?" Basil asks, as if questioning the blade.

"Two bodies… we've all gotta eat. It's not personal." His words have a genuine remorse about them. His knife-bearing hand trembled. "Isn't even for me, the extras. I've got a hungry kid to feed, you see. And I'm sure some of you are good people and I'm sure some of you aren't, but I don't know you and we gotta look out for our own out here. I hate to do this, I really do, so I leave it up to you. Who's it gonna be?"

The group trembles, out of phase, against the back of the dome, murmuring amongst themselves. Basil seems to stand up straighter.

"It's not going to happen." His voice shakes less now. It still shakes, though.

"If it's any consolation, you guys are fucked out here regardless," the Vulture offers. It isn't any consolation.

The Vultures have slowly gathered back behind their flashlight-bearing leader, three of them dragging corpses from within the dome. One of them is empty handed and scratching at his arms with tenacity. The leader raises the silhouette of his blade out of view, flashlight still trained on the cowering crowd.

"Come on, man." The Vulture leader sounds genuinely disappointed. "None of us need this right now." He looks back to the small group of Vultures behind him. "We take only what we need – two of them."

The Vultures don't move, they scratch at their arms and pick at their blackened cuticles.

"Now!" the leader shouts, his voice cracking, eliciting another coughing fit. The four Vulture cronies rush forward at the crowd, which recoils, dispersing. An illogical reaction. There are thirty of us maybe, and only five of them total, but fear is a curious thing.

The following elapses like a film. I watch from behind my eyes, unfeeling, moving automatically, as if on rails. After what feels like an instant I'm staring out a window consisting of parallel bars across a hole in the wall. I'm in the remains of a hotel room, looking out upon the sculpture-ridden courtyard. Through the barred hole, unable to move, I watch the conflict unfold beneath me.

I hear Cass shout my name. My real name. The Vultures begin to tear at my people, with feral tenacity. People who I inspired. People who are here because of me. I watch from behind my eyes.

Muriel Pact, an ex-con turned internet-famous chef is the first to clash with a Vulture, one Benjamin Rhodes, a Machine Learning specialist who had been sent off to the Wasteland some three years before. Benjamin slashes at Muriel with dark extended fingernails. She notes no malice in his eyes, but fear, desperation, as she weaves around, parrying the rabid onslaught of jagged keratin, her arms crossed defensively, bearing the brunt of the Vulture's rage.

Basil tries in vain to rally a few of his supporters into a viable defensive configuration, using the dome-like sculpture as refuge. There is too much panic for coherence. The burly red-shirt protester runs into the dome for shelter before being run through with half a spear, evidently wrenched off one of the Aphaean statues. His eyes widen, and steam billows from the wound in his stomach as he crumbles at Basil's feet.

"Mine! Mine!" A Vulture hops around, dropping the chunk of spear, and grabs the ex-protester's ankles, dragging him around and out of the dome, navigating her way through the surrounding conflicts with impressive indifference.

Using the red-shirt's corpse as a sort of barrier, Basil recedes further back into the dome-like structure, hiding there with several others who had been in the airship.

"Ohh we're fucked, I don't want to die," moans Vince DeFroe, a content creator who had been at the event to protest. He sits, clutching a leg which he is convinced has been broken in the fall, but is really only fractured. He wears a distinct trench coat and rocks back and forth, arms wrapped around his good leg, face white.

By his side is one Rachel Swan, a long-term RA supporter and volunteer PR specialist for the organization. Crisis's antics had understandably been a nightmare for her. Rachel glares at Vince's fetal form, picking him apart.

"That jacket…" Vince's face somehow turns whiter. He says nothing. "You threw the fucking bottle. This is *entirely* your fault. You selfish shit!"

She begins to strike the man's fractured leg with her palm.

"Shhh," insists Basil. The battle rages on outside the dome, and Cass charges in, bloodied beneath the eye, but still red – the blood, not that it matters. She looks down upon Rachel and Vince's quarrel.

"Come on, it doesn't matter now," Basil says, voice trembling, nowhere near assuaging the onslaught of palm-strikes. Basil's eyes widen as he looks Vince up and down. He feels a detached fury working its way into his slipshod emotional state.

"Enough!" Cass's voice booms, bounding within the dome. Her hands are calloused and steaming. "You see what's going on out there? And you're fighting each other? Politics are over, it's us and them, and we're *fucked* if we don't group up and get out there."

"My leg…" Vince begins before Cass smacks him across the head. She picks the Aphaean spear up off the ground, now somewhat charred, and wipes off a layer of burnt flesh and marble with her shirtsleeve. She winds up and launches the piece of spear towards Basil, the still-steaming piece of artwork whizzing by the scientist and embedding itself in the skull of a Vulture who had been creeping up from behind.

"Follow me," she commands, exiting the dome.

Benjamin and Muriel are still locked in combat,

enveloped in a cloud of dark steam spewing from their respective lacerations. The Vulture's leader has finished coughing and holds the lanky Gabriel LaShunt by the neck, carrying him towards a small sculpture – jagged, bronze and contemporary, likely a criticism of industrialism. Gabriel had been part of the sanitation team at the auditorium, was an action-film buff, and wrote poetry about nature in his free time.

Cass is tackled to the ground by another Vulture, the massive Jan St-Pierre, a professor of economics, who holds a shapeless chunk of marble up, ready to strike. Jan sniffs.

"Not sick?" she asks, rhetorically, because she can smell it, or rather, she can't smell it. She notes the gash beneath Cass's eye. The blood a dark red, but still very much a red, and no steam.

"No time for cooking…" Jan mutters, looking away and dropping the chunk of marble onto the grass by Cass's side, her eyes darting back around to the now defunct Gabriel LaShunt, keeled over on the jagged bronze instrument of death and self-expression. The Vulture leader seems to have left this body behind in pursuit of a new quarry. Jan leaps off of Cass and drags Gabriel's body off into the night.

Cass sees the Vulture's leader step towards the dome, retrieves the shard of spear, and intercepts him. They circle one another, Cass not looking at the blade but at the man's eyes, the blade visible in her peripheral vision, but less important than her opponent's thoughts. She recognizes him from somewhere. The leader spends several seconds clearing his throat, and speaks.

"We've got what we came for. We can leave you. Nobody else has to go down."

"We're fucked anyways..." she says. "Your words." Cass grits her teeth and charges at the Vulture, launching the remains of the Aphaean spear at the coughing figure, who narrowly ducks out of its way. He retorts by throwing his blade at Cass, which catches her off guard and embeds itself into her thigh. This wound does little to slow Cass down though, and she's already barreling towards the lead Vulture, knocking him backwards into a pillar in one of the courtyard's corners. The pillar, which had seen better days, cannot bear the brunt of this impact, and decides that now is as good as time as any to abandon its responsibilities vis-à-vis offering support to the mezzanine above them. With a hearty groan, the structure crumbles upon the head Vulture.

Muriel and Benjamin's mano-a-mano has moved across the garden to the impish statue with the cup, which Muriel ducks behind as Benjamin invests in a furious swipe. Rather than Muriel's head, his hand makes contact with the imp's marble cup and lets out a crunch. The Vulture howls and is tackled from behind by Basil, who throws him right into the statue, Benjamin's face bent over into the imp's hollow skull.

Basil, now numb and shaking, picks up a minimalist statue and drives it down over the back of the Vulture's head. The minimalist statue admittedly might just be a metal box, but it's heavy, and manages to break through Benjamin's skull on Basil's fourth downstroke, driving the Vulture's head deeper and deeper into the imp-statue's hollow skull, until his head is practically fused with the statue's, his body hanging limp.

Jan St-Pierre, Vulture, attempting to sneak away, but having some difficulty dragging Gabriel's steaming corpse, ends up backing up right into a limping and battle-worn Cass, who brandishes the late Vulture leader's blade and uses it to run Jan through the gut.

A single Vulture remains; Anthony Graham, who used to have various streams of passive income (including several automated online stores which re-sold small trendy widgets he'd import in bulk at an obscene premium). Anthony had been with the Vultures for a year and a half. He crawls on the ground, having been perhaps trampled by several of the frightened fallen during their initial absconding from the scene. Some of his automated online stores are still generating revenue, transferred directly into Anthony's seized account.

Basil holds the minimalist sculpture/metal box above his head, trembling ferociously, prepared to end Anthony right then and there, but Cass stops his hand.

"Don't," she says, panting. "He has a lot to tell us first."

Interlude

in which Basil's authority is questioned

Muriel Pact peered into the directionless embers of a near-defunct bonfire. Just beside her, Vince DeFroe, ex-bottle-thrower and resident scapegoat was having an emotional breakdown. Muriel's online cooking show had been called *Hard Boiled*, and her foul-mouthed and irreverent persona had since been widely parodied. Sadly, Muriel had no knowledge of her spike in popularity since her deportation.

Vince's emotional breakdown likely stemmed from his reconsideration of the act of vessel-throwing, or "bottling" Basil during the RA rally. Muriel used to have a non-sequitur segment on *Hard Boiled* where she'd bottle some celebrity impersonator between the appetizer and main courses of a given week's lavish meal.

DeFroe was half-weeping an half-hyperventilating to the point where his sobs could barely escape, building up in his glottis and hovering, tense, before being released in gasps and short bursts of apparent pain. Muriel seemed not to notice.

Basil walked over, face twisted with concern, but certainly not empathy.

"We need to be quieter," he said gently, resting a hand on Vince's trench coat. "We don't know who else could be out there." Vince blubbered for a few seconds before producing something coherent.

"B..but..." he sniffled grotesquely, "*he* spends all day yelling." Vince gestured with his neck towards Anthony Graham, captive Vulture, who alternated between whispering to himself and howling morbidly, and so far had not been useful as source of information in any capacity. "And *he's* a prisoner," Vince whimpered.

"We need him," Basil said softly. Vince stared into the erratic embers, and probably began to replay in his mind the scene of his bottling Basil, the very same man who was currently crouched by his side attempting to seem empathetic and failing, but at least trying, and this memory bore down on Vince's psyche like a ton of bricks or feathers, and an all-encompassing feeling of sheer regret rose up in the back of his throat, blocking out any attempts at future discourse with another round of subdued wailing and increasingly erratic glottal-stopped gasps for air.

Anthony Graham, captive Vulture, was tied to a chair with a bit of old rope found lying around. The rope, repurposed from a rope that lies around to a rope that restrains captive Vultures, surely experienced an upgrade in the grand hierarchy of rope-usage. Anthony's latest fit of howls had subsided. Instead, he muttered to himself and chewed at his lips, labial lacerations sputtering smoke.

The chair to which Anthony was tied was sturdy; it had been found on its side in a far corner of the sculpture garden, posing the question of whether it itself was a sculpture, and therefore intended to be looked at rather than sat on. The Vulture struggled through his sweat, and the fingers of his bound hands picked at their discolored cuticles, which were already mostly gone. A trademark sign of a Vulture, most seasoned inhabitants of the Wasteland knew, were cuticles reduced to smoldering black heaps of clotted and re-clotted blood.

Antony had refused the orange juice box and portion of beans he had been offered, eyes darting about. He had demanded, through nonsensical mutterings and howls, quote: "excess flesh," which Basil had taken a hard stance against, refusing under any circumstances to even discuss the possibility of validating the prisoner's cannibalistic urges in exchange for the prospect of information.

"Where did you take him? I won't ask again." Cass looked crazed as she paced in front of Anthony Graham. The Vulture seemed not to notice her. Basil approached from Cass's side, arms crossed. Several other survivors of the fall stood alongside them, eyeing Anthony. The remainder of the group was scattered across the courtyard, which they had been using as a sort of shelter for the past few weeks.

Several expeditions into the dilapidated Inn Between had yielded some basic resources, some mostly intact tarps, which the group splayed across artworks to create almost adequate protection from the caustic rain. Moving inside wasn't an option, significant sections of the Inn seemed to enjoy collapsing on a whim.

Another group of fallen was sat around the remains of a small bonfire in a nearby corner of the camp, cans of beans upon the embers. Some sucked idly on expired juice boxes, which the Wasteland seemed to have in an abundance disproportionate to anything else. Always orange flavor, for some reason. People kept joking about what they'd do for a swig of artificial apple or grape. Vince blubbered inconsistently in a far corner.

Interlude | 75

Cass took Basil aside.

"You know what he wants." she said "We still have bodies. And what if he knows where Crisis is?"

"I refuse to let him indulge in that." Basil's *No Flesh* policy seemed to be the most sacred of his dogmata for the camp.

"He's going to die, either from lack of food or this fucked up withdrawal. Just kill him if you're not going to feed him. Then we'll never know where they took Crisis."

"*If* they took Crisis," Basil corrected, thinking about how jaded this woman must be in order to speak so casually of offing their prisoner, and then chastising himself for being critical of anyone, considering his own state. The past few weeks had not been kind to Basil. He hadn't slept or ate nearly enough. His face looked sunken and relinquished.

"He wouldn't have just left us." Cass sounded less confident in her stance than she'd have liked. A brief sheet of silence, painted with the quiet sputtering of the nearby bonfire's ashes. Basil's hair had gone grey after the first four days.

"I still don't think you should put him on guard duty tonight," Cass said, craning her neck towards the whimpering Vince by the bonfire.

"Need to set an example. What happened out there doesn't matter anymore. We're in this together."

"It's not about that. He's clearly not stable. And I don't think anyone wants *him* as the only line of defense between us and whatever's out there." Cass slapped a mildly mutated mosquito that had latched onto her forearm and eyed the remains suspiciously.

"Is anyone out here stable? Give the guy a break, we've all done stuff we're not proud of."

No response from Cass.

"I made a decision and it's final, you don't have to like it." Basil continued, and turned away towards the bonfire's remains.

Anthony tired of alternately muttering to himself and picking at his cuticles and so resorted to his strategy of being a complete annoyance by howling as loudly as he could. Everyone had gotten pretty good at ignoring him. The less they seemed affected by it, the sooner he stopped, they found.

9. Succulent

in which Basil confronts Crisis, and Cass acquires crucial information

Basil awoke to the harsh pitter patter of acid rain eating away at the tarmac over his head. A few hours of sleep, he supposed. There had been worse nights. The young doctor rose and glanced over at the usual guard station, expecting genuinely to see a vigilant Vince. Instead, emptiness. Basil was appalled. This is what he gets for giving second chances. What if someone else had noticed Vince's absence? Basil would certainly have to answer for this gaff. I signed up for this, he told himself, lazily wandering to the absent watch post.

Basil scanned the area. Vince was nowhere to be seen. What if he had up and left? And with one of their only flashlights, too. Fuck. His heart raced with responsibility. He felt alive.

Across the camp, blanketed by dusk, Cass creeped towards the rusted dome. She had once been tasked with reprimanding a group of infected, back in the quarantine zone. Her weapon had "jammed" and the family has escaped. In retrospect, her mistake was not a matter of compassion, but one of pride. A refusal to carry out orders she disagreed with, ideologically. She felt a similar lack of compassion as she crouched in the corpse-ridden dome, which smelled oddly of chicken, and sawed off a Tar-stained arm with the remains of the sculpted Aphaean spear.

A light, unmistakable, from several floors up. Basil noticed it after some pacing. Was Vince really unstable enough to wander up into the fractured depths of Inn Between? Basil grabbed the flashlight and the blade the Vultures had left behind, stowed them in his belt, and grabbed an expired juice box for the road. He winced as he sucked the foul liquid down, squeezing the box to expedite the process.

Basil had only been inside the Inn under cover of daylight, but rules were made to be broken, and fears are to become comforts. And Basil did feel a sort of detached comfort, a sense of control as he hopped up the concrete steps in the Inn's entryway, thinking about chastising Vince, the coward, whom Basil was now certain he could not trust.

As Basil crossed the threshold into the Inn's uninviting hall, his ears were subjected to another howl, followed by shouting. Basil felt an almost-forgotten rush of adrenaline. They had been few and far between, those soothing natural highs released when his brain felt danger. It had taken more and more to set them off. He smiled and appreciated the twisting sensation of fear in his stomach.

These howls came from deeper within the Inn, several floors up, rattling the hotel's anatomical correlate of a ribcage. Basil felt cold and absent as he trudged up the stairs.

Anthony tore into the disembodied arm as though it were one of the giant medieval-style turkey legs they used to have at Disney, before the Disney Incident. He emanated a satisfied shudder, eyes rolled back, face contorted, communicating a sense pleasure that looked a lot like surprise. The cuticle-picking ceased, and hands fell limp within their constraints at the back of the chair. Cass held the arm out in front of the Vulture, watching him indulge with a jaded sense of interest.

The Vulture's eyes rolled forward, fixed on the arm, widening as he prepared to jump in for another series of bites. His teeth gnashed upon empty air, as Cass's own arm

80 | TAR

recoiled, taking the mildly masticated disembodied arm along with it. Anthony froze, in shock, and seemed to be preparing to recommence the howling.

"Make a fucking noise and you'll never get another taste. Talk," she commanded, glancing behind. Anthony's eyes scrolled from the disembodied arm to meet Cass's no-nonsense gaze. He smiled appreciatively.

Basil navigated Inn Between's halls with care, taking large steps over missing segments of floor. Chunks of the ground came away behind him as he crept through the halls toward the source of the howls. The deeper he ventured, the thicker the air became.

A faint glow through peeling wallpaper from just around the corner. Vince's flashlight; stained and still warm, upon investigation. It smelled oddly familiar. More charcoal stains graced what little remained of the floor's carpet, appearing to stretch off into the bowels of the hall. Basil pressed on, absent-mindedly following the stain, watching his step.

Basil happed upon a door which had been halved with no great precision. It stood at knee-level, splintered wood jutting upwards like uneven crystal.

"Vince?" Basil asked aloud, inquiring into the void

of the dark room. He had never been this far into the Inn before. Basil's flashlight danced across a full-looking wardrobe sat in a far corner. The room was otherwise entirely devoid of furnishing. This was unusual, even for Inn Between, where the remains of chairs and beds sat in rooms, having nowhere else to go.

Something inside Basil once would have screamed at him to leave this place, some bygone system of premonition. Nothing did. He wandered through the seemingly vacant chamber, unfeeling but not oblivious to the implied danger, hand hovering by the blade in his belt. The air was thick with dust.

"Bless you for visiting, Trespasser. Must have been hard to get in." The words were incredibly clear, though the voice was cracked and hoarse. The voice had come from behind, though, from the corner closest to the room's entrance.

"There's barely a door," Basil mustered, turning around. Basil was performing his trademark move where he believes he's doing a much better job at hiding his nerves than he actually is.

"Barely a door indeed. The entrance crumbled, the windows barred. Very few visitors, Trespasser, on this hallowed hardwood, the Trial's trail." The stranger's voice scraped the ground at Basil's feet. The speaker was stood facing the corner, by the door. Basil thought about correcting the creature, explaining that both the door and windows, while in bad shape, were easily traversable – as in the remains of a door could be stepped through with ease, Basil having done so about thirty seconds prior.

"How long have you been here?" Basil asked, glancing through the window at something burning just outside. The group's bonfire, surely. Might be a good emergency means of escape, the window. The creature turned around, a light smog engulfed its claws, spewing from what were once cuticles. A left thumb rose like a pickaxe, bearing down into the volcanic soil between index finger and index fingernail, the skin seeming never to quite recede nor regenerate, held at bay, going nowhere, billowing.

"Orange juice?" the stranger asked, his words dancing precarious across vocal fissures. A cracked hand reached out from the smog, holding out a juice box. "Not that you could drink it, Apparition." The lone stranger had long, knotted black hair, greasily crawling down the back of his head and sticking to his neck. He looked wet, and as though he should smell offensively. The parts of his neck that were visible through the damp strands of hair were a sickly white, bulging veins tinted black with Tar.

"Look, I'm not here to hurt you. We have food, we can help," said Basil.

"Food?" The stranger wandered past Basil and looked out the window. "Down at the camp? The camp that I created? It's imaginary, Basil. There's nobody else out here. Not even you. And keep the howling down, if you would, I implore you, let us sleep, Apparition."

"It's you, Elliot." Basil caught himself smiling with recognition. "You don't think I'm real?"

"Call me Crisis."

"You don't think I'm real?" Basil repeated, amused. In retrospect, Basil would have kicked himself for the depraved pleasure he took from meeting Crisis in such a state. The interaction felt like a sort of victory for Basil. He had outlasted his inspiration, had become better than his idol after all, felled a god through sheer attrition. He would not call him Crisis.

"You *were* real, Apparition. You amused me, you thought you could do what I did so well. But nobody's left now, and it's my fault, I left you all, my people, my followers, to die, hence the trial." Crisis gestured at his surroundings, as though it were evident there was a trial taking place. All Basil saw were the wretched remains of a room that was once quite hospitable, in another life.

Smoke emanated from between the wardrobe's charred doors. There was nothing even vaguely suggestive of a trial.

Crisis chuckled.

"Yes, in due time," he said, not to Basil.

"Is Vince here?" Basil's voice quaked with naïveté.

"Trespassers contribute." Crisis said absentmindedly. He seemed locked in conversation with someone else.

"Who are you talking to?" Basil asked in earnest.

"Athena," Crisis said. "The real one, Basil, not just someone with the same name. She's always handled these sorts of things. That's why I can't leave." Crisis stood between Basil and the half-door.

"It's been weeks. What have you been eating?" Basil was inching backwards, glancing back out the window at the bonfire and catching a quick glance of the captive Anthony, who hadn't howled in almost an hour.

"We have some beans...if you're hungry." Basil said.

"Obsolete," Crisis smiled, his pickaxe-thumbs moving on to the pinkies. A brief silence, not awkward so much as tense. Crisis' eyes widened. "You've come to punish me. Like Philomela. Surely. Is that why you mean to feed me? Will you feed me my children? Will you become a bird, Trespasser? *Metamorphose??*" Crisis's voice trailed off into further incomprehensible references to ancient myth, and he stepped in front of the half-door, blocking the way out. His face was monstrous, black veins twisting across the whites of his eyes.

"How did you get in?" Crisis asked. "The gates to my court have been sealed for the duration of the trial". Crisis spoke frantically, slurring his words. "Tell me!" he shouted.

Basil took a step back, holding his knife up in front of him. Noting Crisis's apparent instability. Was this the same man who had inspired him? The same man from the posters and the songs? No. Crisis was over, this was someone else. Basil repeated this to himself internally.

"The door was open," spoke Basil, softly and deliberately, "I just walked in." Crisis laughed, it was a disturbing high-pitched cackle that seemed forced.

"That's impossible. The gate was sealed, I was standing trial… the fates…" Crisis trailed off again, wandering into a corner of the room and waving his hands around in the air. Basil was horrified, though the strange sense of validation in seeing Crisis so far gone persisted. He himself had his mind intact and his knife trained, he thought, proudly.

"What have you been eating?" Basil's voice cracked and his hand tensed up, cramping. It took a strong concerted effort to keep the knife from falling from his grip. It vibrated in his shaking hand along with his wavering voice.

Crisis gave Basil a disappointed look, and gestured towards the wardrobe. "I think we both know what I've been eating, kid."

The two former leaders of the Radical Altruists circled one another. Crisis baring his nails and teeth, and Basil his knife. There was nothing the least bit altruistic about the situation.

Crisis took a deep breath through his nose

"Do you smell that?" he asked. Basil had noted the smell earlier – it was entirely dyssynchronous. Crisis looked as though he should smell putrid, and the wardrobe... the closet which Basil was sure harbored Vince's corpse, among others, emanated a familiar odor.

"There's nothing else in the world, once you try it." The Crisis cocked his head to the side and produced a small blade from his pocket, holding it out, his arm shook unconsciously.

"It's unlike anything you could even imagine," Anthony said to Cass, now impossibly placid, hands limp, "and it's abundant, if you know where to look. There's all this perfectly viable food, everywhere. The catch is, once you get into it, there doesn't seem to be much getting out. But we make decisions, and we try not to kill. You can disagree

Succulent | 87

with us, you can try to be morally superior and refuse to eat the stuff, but that's because you're still thinking in the old framework, as if things are the same out here as they are in the cities. And it's not like that, it's clearly different. You need to adapt."

"We're not animals," Cass spoke softly.

"We are. I saw what you did to Stone. He wasn't a bad guy, you know. The stuff about his kid, that was all true."

"That was –" Cass recoiled.

"Jeremy Stone, ex-European cola mogul. You crushed him to death. Waste of perfectly good meat. He was a decent guy, would have wanted us to have it," the Vulture sighed. "With each passing week you survive you'll understand us a little bit more, and it took me months before I gave in. But once you do... well you can't really stop for too long. And you best not eat it too quickly either, without a good tolerance built up. You'll end up in another world."

"It's... *cannibalism.*" Cass no longer felt like she was the one in control.

"You say that like it's a dirty word," said Anthony.

"It is."

"No dirtier than expired beans and juice boxes. Only orange, too, right? What a sick joke. The meat is cooked you know. From the inside out. We had a few scientists with us when we fell. Their theory was that our bodies have some active processes working hard to maintain a normal internal temperature, despite the intense heat of the Tar. But once you die, see, the body can't regulate this temperature anymore, and the Tar cooks you from the inside out. Have you smelled any infected bodies? Not what you'd expect, right? Almost like..."

"Chicken," Cass whispered. Anthony smiled.

"But chicken's never made you feel like this," Anthony whispered back, eyes transfixed by the remains of the arm Cass held, just out of the reach of his jowls.

"I'll give you the rest if tell me where you've taken Crisis," she demanded. Anthony smiled again, still eyeing the arm.

"Food first," Anthony demanded back.

"One more bite," decided Cass, with hesitancy. She watched intently as Anthony bore into the arm's tender flesh, the juices staining his mouth as though he were a child eating a disembodied arm filled with blackcurrant.

"Up there," Anthony said, cocking his head to the side to gesture towards the nearby building. "He ran off as soon as the fighting started. I recognized him from the TV, back in the day. Doesn't look like he used to." Cass dropped the remains of the arm on the ground and walk back towards the camp. Anthony shouted after her:

"And I've seen him there. Since then, in the window! When you're busy playing community! He's been up there watching!" Anthony cackled. "He ran away! Almost instantly!" Once Cass was out of earshot his smile quickly dissipated. His laughs quieted as he caught his breath, slumped over in his chair, closed his eyes, and allowed himself to be swept away by sensation.

Crisis was alone now, playing with his blade, and wandered over to the steaming wardrobe, unthinking. Not hungry but wanting very much to eat.

"Do you remember my speech?" Basil was there again.

"Apparition..." Crisis began, absentmindedly, and inched closer to the wardrobe.

"Tar doesn't make you like this, remember? You're not a monster." Basil inched towards the door, eyes locked on Crisis.

"I very much am, Apparition, I very much am." Crisis opened the wardrobe doors, allowing most of Vince's torso to crumble out. Basil could see remains of a few more bodies behind, stacked haphazardly in the wardrobe. Crisis paused pensively, and for a moment seemed strangely lucid. He continued: "A monster who gave people hope, a monster who rallied people, who fed off of their adoration. And they *adored* me, Apparition, you adored me too. Really, I was always feeding off people, it was the only thing that made me happy, satisfied – it was the love, the affection. People did anything and everything for me. This is no different. But I can change, I can start over. We have everything we need, now that you're all gone." Crisis looked back over to Basil, who had almost made it to the door.

"Keep you knife trained, Trespasser." Crisis's bout of lucidity had come to an abrupt close, and he once again donned a curtain of detachment as a makeshift cape.

"The man I knew died weeks ago," Basil said to himself, "this is just a shell."

"Just a shell," he repeated, blade quivering.

10. Imbroglio

as told by Crisis, a broken man with a fractured mind

Why do people have to read so much into everything? Crisis is in a room, call me Crisis, I'm in a room, what a dreadful name for a character, Crisis, it brings nothing new to the table, but how do you imagine this room? The space of this story is yours, not mine, and my role is vaguely religious in my providing you a framework to mold and interpret like a self-reflexive gospel made of unsettled clay.

I wonder what showers feel like. Call me Crisis, how horrible it is to think about mirrors, since so many have had these thoughts already. Mirrors have already been exploited, my reaction to my own twisted figure as it stares back at me is frankly more depressing due to the shrewdness of the image than due to my ghastly appearance. The ghastlier the better out here it would seem.

Are you paying attention? Is attention enough? I was alert, I was there when they dropped us. I watched hell unfold from behind the blast door of my skull. I tried so hard to make a difference. The visitors did too. I've done bad things, I've done very bad things to survive.

They'll be here soon, and you'll get to meet them. The others who survived. Basil will come to punish me. We were both wrong, really, to be crude. The only way to lead effectively is to abandon the self, and become a vessel. They say the best writing is impersonal as in without self as in I am the vessel as in I shattered and rained down light in shards across your world bless you.

People never read into things enough, there's so much beneath the surface, beneath my surface, emptiness call me Crisis, call me Elliot, I am hell, I am god, have you tasted it? The gospel of flesh, the pretension of being, the ideological cannibalism of leading, inciting worship, feeding off of them, starry-eyed and desperate for ideology, counterculture. As if truth was something that most had missed but they had caught a glimpse of through maybe just the suspicion that everyone was wrong, but what kind of a premise is that?

Have you tasted it? The light-footed beast that paces inches beneath the surface. The crippled chimera,

Imbroglio | 93

the collective unconscious. If only you understood it, so subjective in nature but surely objectively *the best ever*, really, nothing compares, a category of its own, the taste, and the feeling, somehow, even better. Beyond. Imagine spending your whole life thinking you were *feeling* only to learn that what you thought was *feeling* was a cheap correlate – knockoff sensation.

It is a shame we cannot yet record and reproduce experience. "Being" being such nonsense, as it were. If I could share the taste, the sensation, then you'd understand, otherworldly. I have everything I need here, Crisis, call me that, please, bless you, welcome, friends. Lovely of you to have gotten in past all the rubble in the doorway, such commitment to our cause, friends, lovers, have a seat, look at all I've curated, have a juice box, only orange left, and lightly expired, I'm afraid.

No, I won't tell you what the walls look like, a ridiculous request – outlandish – just look. Have a seat, you're here, be present, please. Orange juice? Fresh out, I'm afraid. I'll ask Athena if she can get more. A nickname? No, the real Athena. The original, Blasphemer. Only kidding. About the blasphemy, that is. She's laid back for a goddess, considering. Not joking about her presence, I said. Here for the trial, of course, the legal kind, not like a test, although I suppose they are comparable.

Will the accused please be seated. Rise within, maybe. Don't. Orange juice? You really ought to accept, my guest, transformed to a bird by now, surely, I can see him through the window. Metamorphosis is a curious thing. Tastes like chicken. You can't imagine what it would feel like to fly, but birds can't imagine what it would feel like not to fly. Sensation is wasted on the acclimated, on the sensitized. This is different. You've never felt like this before. You never will. That's more tragic than any transforming trespassers who might sully my sensation, though they've paid their dues, as I've paid mine. As ever-present as they are ephemeral, they fuel the feeling fire in turn.

What terrible decisions we've made for ourselves, we had no say, really, couldn't have stopped it. It wouldn't have happened if we could have, and it happened, oh how it happened, you can feel it, can't you? I am a fleeting thought in the mind-analogue of a greater being, and my digressions spawn universes. Equal parts omnipotent and insignificant: a fly on the wall is God to the universe inside the fly, but only a fly on the wall to the world within the walls, surely, as are you, listener; creator. The tree falling in the forest makes a sound once you think about it. But it didn't exist until you did.

It was self-defense, surely, as with the others. They sustained me, prolonged my trial, lengthened my thread. This was my punishment – to live upon our rockface, berated by waves. Here comes one now: it dances, sputtering, and burrows its way into my chest.

11. Ashes

as experienced by Cass, the reluctant leader left of the aftermath

"We tend not to eat the head. It's different from a goat or something. Eating the head is a bit much, and not worth the emotional hassle. There isn't much meat on it either."

It had been a few hours since Anthony had eaten and he was beginning to lightly scrape at his cuticles, feeling out the groundwork, planning the next cutaneous excavation. The Vulture's newly softened temperament had caught the attention of most of the camp as they awoke with the sun. They sat around his chair, listening intently as he described the finer aspects of endocannibalism, as he described it, which means only eating people from inside one's own social group. Vultures, he explained, expected to be eaten after their deaths, giving back what they have taken, as it were. When possible, they subsist only on fellow Vultures,

Anthony explains to the wide-eyed audience, thanking the bodies before indulging. It's all carried out with a considerable level of respect. What happened earlier was unfortunate. Desperate.

"So avoiding the heads is also a matter of respect, sort of, the head is one's main identifier, usually – if the head remains untouched, the identity can outlive the body. The legacy can last a little bit longer."

"The legacy of being a disembodied head..." someone interjected.

"You can't win 'em all." Anthony smiled.

The word *decapitate* comes from the Latin *caput*, meaning head, the same root that's brought us the likes of *capital*, *captain*, and *cap*. That's not to be confused with the German *kaput*, meaning broken, finished, over; though the two often go hand in headless hand. For example, when Basil Hollister's disembodied head flew out the looming window of Inn Between and landed just next to Anthony's chair, it would have been accurate to say that Basil was both *kaput* and that he had been *decapitated*.

Cass had been pacing some ways away from the group when the head fell. Her thoughts had not been racing. It was not a competition. Perhaps her thoughts jogged, or power-walked. She worked through the situation deliberately and in no particular rush. Crisis had abandoned them. His people, his followers. Because, at the end of the day, any member of the RA was surely a follower of Crisis, whether or not they'd admit it to themselves. Basil sure as hell was, and she was too, she admitted, after some soft self-coercion. It was around then in the mind-jog that she heard the screams. Not Anthony, she thought, who was surely still placated by his snack. Someone else, multiple people now.

Stone's kid. The thought was thrust into her mind unannounced. The leader of the Vultures, whom she had killed. Cass could see his face, the kid's, in Jeremy's arms on the cover of some shitty magazine.

She felt nothing when she saw the head. Cass's only real feeling was the feeling that she should be feeling something. That, and a creeping sense of inevitability. Guilt? Maybe. For breaking Basil's rules? For working so hard to get Crisis to the event in the first place? There was no time for that sort of paralyzing sentiment, Cass thought, in a surge of practicality. She had joined the police force because there were rules, and people needed to enforce those rules. Anthony was right, the rules were different out here, but whatever they were, they sure as fuck don't allow you to decapitate your successors. It had to be Crisis up there, she thought. A cold rage pulsed through her. She didn't feel angry – it wasn't that crude – the anger simply was. She was its agent. She had work to do, a purpose. It was relieving.

Crisis had presumably eaten the rest of Basil, she thought, and felt a tinge of disgust – not the emotion, just a physical response in her stomach. It was her body's way of notifying her she should be disgusted by the prospect of her ex-lover and bona fide hero subsisting on the flesh of his admirers.

They had to go in after him. Surely. There were enough of them. It wasn't even a question. And they'd listen to her if she told them to, Cass reasoned. But what would that make her? A leader? A dirty word out here, surely. She'd seen enough of them fall, or worse. Cass wrestled with the paradox: the people who want to be in charge, the ones who *know for a fact* that they are best for the job, that they know best; these were not the types of people who Cass thought should be in charge. How can you possibly know what's best for everyone if you think that you know what's best for everyone?

I won't tell them what to do, she thought, calmly, wandering back into the metal dome to find the worn down Aphaean spear, which had gotten some pretty violent mileage for something meant only to serve as sculpture.

Everything went cold again as she dragged the spear back to the group, who were huddled around Anthony's chair, murmuring.

Cass began to speak, allowing her words to be chosen for her, by that cold unfelt rage that *was*. A call to arms, or something more hesitant? She said "if" a lot and made some short-term promises regarding food and shelter. "If we so choose," and "if it were up to me." She resonated, maybe, with these people. But they were beyond choosing. They'd have done anything she barked, she thought. This notion, the notion of control elicited in her another physiological disgust response. Again Cass was puzzled about its origin. She spoke, still, her unconscious words clawing their way through the thick, underpopulated air, tunneling through earholes, vibrating stereocilia, and sending signals bounding into broken brains, laying root and branching out. Viral. The bonfire's embers gasped and sputtered in the distance, a display that reeked of finality, but smelled more like smoke.

Printed in Great Britain
by Amazon